i

Astitva Prakashan

Bilaspur, Chhattisgarh 495001
First Published by Astitva Prakashan 2021
Copyright © Pausali Mukherjee 2021
All Rights Reserved.
ISBN: 978-93-91219-03-1

VERSOFICTION

PAUSALI MUKHERJEE

ABOUT THE AUTHOR

Pausali Mukherjee, born and brought up in 'The City of Joy-- Kolkata', the author, a Postgraduate in English Literature and Language, is a dedicated educationist for more than a decade. She believes in the power of pen; "Pen can wound, Pen can heal too"-- that's what she says. She likes to portray the picture with words and paint them with the colour of words only. She is a true Wordsmith. Few of her literary works have recently been published in the Anthologies named "The Soul Talks" and "The Lightening Flies". And a collection of her Twenty-Five Poems has recently been published as a solo book under the name of "Flip to Fillip" from Notion Press Publication House. Readers may find her quotes in Google too.

ABOUT THE BOOK

This is a literary mash up of Verse and Fiction. This is the author's second solo project divided into three parts.

Part one named as Milangé is a collection of 25 poems on miscellaneous themes.

Part two named as Unfinished Fairytales is a collection of 28 poems only on the theme of broken or incomplete love.

Part three is a bit different as it is a collection of 9 Mini-tales on various themes named under Big Shorts. Altogether there are 62 literary pieces named uniformly as VERSOFICTION.

WORDS OF THANKSGIVING

I would like to thank Almighty for keeping the flame of creativity within me constantly burning. Thank you Almighty for keeping me safe and sound and making my mind and pen to move ahead and create something new each day for the world of literature.

Sincere Thanks to my parents, younger brother and all my supporters, friends, colleagues and readers. You all motivate me to push my pen forward in every moment to write something for you to read.

A special thanks to **Mr. Sanjeev Kulhari** and the entire team of **Daffodils World School** for their continuous encouragement and kind words of appreciation. Those are always so motivating.

And most importantly my heartiest thanks to

Mr. Vikram Singh Thakur for his concern for my work and paving its way to publish through

Astitva Prakashan. Thanks to the entire team of

Astitva Prakashan for their ceaseless support and guidance.

DEDICATION

This book I dedicate to my Late Grandparents,
Late Mr. Balaram Chandra Chatterjee
Late Mrs. Bharati Chatterjee
Late Mr. Satyajiban Mukherjee
Late Mrs. Mrinalini Mukherjee

TABLE OF CONTENT

PART-I MELANGÉ

PART-II THE UNFINISHED FAIRYTALES

PART- III BIG SHORTS

PART-I

MELANGÉ

Collection of Twenty-Five Poems on miscellany themes

EVENING WALK

The tranquillity of the time was tormented.
The only one thought throughout prevailed.
Which since centuries we fought!
Were those wars really needed?

The path on my evening walk,
Which my feet keep back on the track,
Isn't the same one through which,
Since the starting the Civilisation walk?

Homo Habilis evolved into Sapiens.
Palaeolithic changed into Nuclear age-
But what still kept unturned among us,
Is the eternal flame of opposition and rage.

Earth's Seven Tectonic Plates,
We pieced into unnumbered borders.
Just to stop being intrude or invade-
By our own, known as "Others".

Assimilating the white pieces for ages,
The Prophets are threading Love.
Does Peace arrive ever at all but!
With the flapping wings of the Dove?

Why should we tell our children!
Those prolonged tales of valour?

Where, boxed bodies with bunch of medals,
We gift each other as an ultimatum of war!

A world where exist the word 'all for all',
Perhaps we never ever wanted to build.
Neither we wanted to shut the profit-shop of war,
Nor wanted the soldierism to be abolished!

With every passing day,
With the weary sunset ray,
My Evening Walk concludes,
In such an unsorted way.

Lot many questions
With uncountable "Whys",
UTOPIA, UNICORN and UBUNTU
They are not only an imagination, rather, BIG FAT
LIES.

WILL YOU?

Hello..!
Will you take my poetry?
Will you take it for free?
I am not selling it at all
Yes, please believe me.

Who am I ?

I am the penner
I am the author
I am the fuel
Of my paper generator.

I am the fool who guessed; thought
Through the pen
Magic can be made
Change can be brought.

I am the human
Honoured for failures
To be born as a brainchild
Of brainless business.

In the world of sell
Worth gets no price gross
Art weighs on the scale
Of the profit and loss.

Hence here on road
I dispense for free
All the parts of my mind
All my poetry.

You can crumble these pieces
Into crumpled paper
And trash it into the bin
Where you just threw
The cold can of tin

Being the creator
I can bear the pain
To see the debris
Once, creation of my pen.
But neither I can control my mind
Nor I can be a wise part
To stop thinking and penning down
Or trading the value of art.

So I am dispensing for free
All my poetry
You can trust and take
I won't charge a single penny.
Will you ?

LET THE DEVIL SLEEP

They made the devil in them, sleep a long time back--
Don't poke them to again arouse it.
You will be tired trying them in all battlefield,
I bet, everywhere you will conquer defeat.

The devil in them is like a volcano,
It sleeps but never can be tamed.
It erupts when it awakes,
And make its enemies framed.

So, better not to mock their generosity,
Who made their devils slumbered.
Let rest their devils in eternal peace,
Their patience shouldn't be lumbered.

VICTORY OF ILLUSION

May be they are nowhere in our lives,
We form a bubble of illusion.
But the high time never comes
To pin the bubble.
And let go in vain all our imagination.
It might be our imagination,
But not infatuation for sure.
It was Love;
It was, It is and It will be.
Victorious forever.
As true as the ray of The Sun.
It is an announcement
Of the Victory of our illusion.

FLIP THE COIN

———◆———

We have burnt her forest, garbaged her ocean,
Polluted her air with the smoke of our civilisation,
Blocked her growth with our rolling wheels of motion,
And kept ourselves boasting on our occasions of
invention.

We were enjoying and were filled with so much of 'Us',
We forgot our limit and so drunk for all our successful
phenomena,
That to quench our unending thirst, then we invented a
Virus,
And the way was unique to welcome CORONA.

Our investment on the invention proved wrong,
It shook us from our very core,
Our weapon acted against us as a Boomerang,
GOD and Nature together laughed with a roar.

If you flip the coin and look at the other side,
There lies another part of the story,
Among the worldwide pandemic you will find the
joyride,
Which nature is enjoying now with an enormous glory.

Perhaps, our Father in Heaven has made this plan,
That We, His best created creatures only will destroy our
clan.

By the time our Mother Nature will heal her wounds and
remove the thorns,
Because again She has to resurrect and give birth to the
new unborns.

A LETTER

Dear King,
The time has arrived
To be the king.
Dear King,
The Time has arrived,
Just not to achieve,
But to accept too.
For being accepted
As the King.

Dear King,
The time has arrived
To mix all the colours
And to paint the canvas with White.

Dear King
The time has came for you to learn,
That the true colour of love is white.
It is a gathering of hundred hue together.

Dear King,
Time is knocking you
To let yourself lit in that glow of hundred hue.
And to whiten yourself into that sacred serenity.

Dear King,
Time is saying,

The war for which You are honoured,
It is time for you now
To love the warriors of that war.

Dear King,
The time has arrived
Be The King,
Not just A Ruler.
If not today!
Then when?
If not today,
Then tomorrow will never come.

Dear King,
We, the subject of your kingdom
The kingdom, your object of leisure.
The leisure, fills you with pleasure.
Those 'We' wish, if you hear the whisper of time.
Those 'We' wish, if you transform your soul.
Those 'We' wish, if you wish to remain you
remembered.
Those 'We' wish,
That "if" may happen with you soon.
That "if" should happen with you soon.

FALL

————◆————

Few celebrate the season of 'Fall'.
Not only because it brings Autumn.
Neither because it's a month of love for some.
But because it brings shower.
Shower of blessings.
Blessings for few and fewer lives.

It may bless few,
With a refuge which shelters,
A refugee like me, you!
At the end of all wars.
Wars we prepare-
To fight daily and forever.
With ourselves, with us.

In the disguise of a butter doll,
'Fall' may have blessed few,
With a butterfly of happiness,
Whose babbles brings smile,
And bursts them into laughter,
In their lonely dusks of slumber,
When they bleed after a day's fight,
In their coop of eight by eight.

'Fall' has blessed few,
With some mesmerizing eyes,
At a glance which might brighten,

Their time and smiles.
Whose soothing fragrance,
Might soothe their souls!
But who hurried too much,
To inscribe their names-
In the cold tombstones.
But still whose presence,
Is like the aroma of clove,
Makes feel of being complete,
In the hemisphere of lost love.

'Fall' has blessed few,
With some blessed meetings.
'Fall' has let few, found a host,
In those every nooks of life,
Where they thought, they are lost.
'Fall' has blessed few,
To rise after every fall,
To re-discover then re-toil.

This is not an "Ode to Autumn",
The season of 'Fall'.
When leaves leave their place,
To be back again overall.
To re-appear as new,
In their apparel of green hue.
Rather grant this Ode,
For those special all
Who being gifted specially,
Celebrate 'Fall'.

FURNACING THE FURNISHING

Some stories are written with pencil,
It can be erased and re-written.
But beneath the imprint of the new pencil mark,
As an inscription the old stories remain.

Tide of Time can wash people away,
From the shore of our life sea.
But no Tsunami can ever wash out,
The gripping strong roots of their memory.

In such Coming and Going and Happening and Re-
happening,
Life takes its shape.
'Canapés' called life, get toppings of wisdom
Where Experience acts as a chef.

Through the chores of the course of life,
Fate keeps its wheel of fire turning.
Human clay turns into a terracotta
The furnishing ends in furnacing.

With the ink of occurrences,
Pottery of life keeps penning a Poetry,
Where new comes and turns old,
But in that eternal novelty,
The essence of old retains in bold.

DEMOCRACY

———◆———

Under the crooked red eyes of rules,
Under the monarchic umbrella of Don'ts and Dos
If your brain is signalling you,
To proceed like-
Thinking before Acting.
Then you are carrying,
A Democracy within yourself.
Relish and cherish that Democrat in you.
Because you don't need a country to prove
Your Democratic desires.
A country never nurture a Democratic mind,
It can't rather !
All you need is just your thought process.
Thought process, your, very own.
Remove the shackles of century old prejudices.
The toxic orthodoxies which pull you back to the puddle,
Puddle full with hypocrisy and fake.
Which just like a poisonous piece of cake,
Can ruin, can spoil an entire entity entirely, eternally.
It is you who can carry Democracy,
Within you, with you.
Just be aware of the Fakes,
Under the masquerade carrying
Friendly bodies but autocratic soul.
Rest is fine.
Dear Democracy-
Cheer up!

MANNEQUIN

A black hooded jacket of Anguish,
With a grey denim of Fear.
A red pleaded chiffon of Hypocrisy,
With a blue brooch of Compare.
A purple cap of Hesitation,
With a golden clutch of Vanity in hand.
A pink spaghetti top of Lust,
With a slice of Greed as a yellow headband.

So many emotions,
So many feelings.
Seem as the apparels, so strange!
Variety of dresses show,
Plenty of shades.
Following the formula of change.

To hide the real ugly nakedness,
Behind the decor of masquerades.
We, keep the clothes put on and off,
Like your thousands thoughts—gallop!
We, the Mannequin, the doll king and queen,
Of the designer dazzling showcase.
Replicating somehow in our structured self,
The frame made with bone and flesh.

MAY I...!

———◆———

I do not wish to lock,
My hand in hand
To run another same day
With that clock hand.
I don't wish to think,
For another next day.
Where round and round
Goes the game of
Lost and Found.
I don't wish to splash
The mud of monotony
From the big bog
Of the conceptualized disharmony.

I want to laugh out loud,
Whenever I wish to.
And not explaining
The cause, why?
I want to get whatever I demand
If not got, then cry.

I want to roam around
In the kingdom of dreams,
In the beauty sleep hours.
With such plain eyelids.

I want to wake up with
No worries to be alarmed.
Next morning, with the cacophony
With that fix hour clocked.

I want to walk back
Not down the memory lane
But to reverse the revolving earth
And live my childhood again.
"May I...!"

FLY OVER

He saw a flock of birds
Flying over his head.
He guessed those were vultures
The birds of dead.

From the point he looks up
Life seems husk.
Dawn, Day, Noon or Full moon,
All alike dusk.

In the world he lives
Words rust.
With end number of shoes
And their greyish dust.
His childish eyes
Have experience captured.
Aged six decades may be
Broken and ruptured.

You may find him
If you widen your vision.
Ageing under a Flyover
In a motionless ocean.

HOMECOMING

It's Spring.
Marks the end of Winter.
It's Spring.
Marks the end of a journey,
Known as Migration.
And then rest for few days,
To start again after recovery.
It's Spring.
The time of
The Homecoming.
Or The Homecoming
Always be granted
As the Spring!

Are you ever away from home?
For being duty bound!
To Nation, To Profession,
To Them or to Self?
Then you may realize
The hidden desire
The eager flapping
Of the wings of the migratory birds?
To reach home soon
After each passing Winter.
How the way of three hours or days,
Seems as three decades.
To see the shine of those bright faces.

Keep your way to gaze.
Then you may realize.
That you bring with you,
A whole box full of joy and stories,
For those innocent curiosity's sleep tales.
Those joy are not purchased
With mere piece of printed paper,
But with your deepest urge
To see the twinkle of those eyes,
To see the glossy cheeks of happiness.
It's Spring.
The time of
The Homecoming.
Or The Homecoming
Always be granted
As the Spring!

It's Spring
The best season for-
The lucky home comer.
But few are there.
Their journeys stopped forever.
Journey known as 'Life'.
Who are God's chosen few,
Whom He loves the most.
He calls them in this Spring.
To complete the eternal circle
Of their Final Homecoming.
It's Spring.
The time of
The Homecoming.
Or The Homecoming

Always be granted
As the Spring!

REBEL

The more you harp
The more I bleed
The more I grow stronger

The more you preach
The more I disobey
The more I cool my anger

The more you rule
The more I unfollow
The more I drive towards danger

The more you scare
The more I sooth
The more my mind gets pleasure

I am a rebel
You don't know me
For you, I am a stranger.
(15)
SHE
You can prove
Your worst
But still she will
Always trust

You can show

Your red rage
But she will
Stand there
Without a back thrust

She will hold your arm
In time of your fall
Whether you are or not
Hold hers back
When she expects
If the wind of time ever gust

She can fight
All battles in and out
To protect you from omens
She will make room
Even in her womb
To keep away the blazing heat
To avoid the dirt of dust

The eternal bond
Tied by Almighty
Seems always invisible
But when in the daylight
While entering through her dark door
Heard your first cry,
Visibility of the Umbilical Chord
How can the world distrust ?

DAMSEL

———◆———

I will tell you a story

A story of a damsel
A damsel not for sell

A damsel not in distress
A damsel not in stress

A damsel of dignity
A damsel of responsibility

A damsel in space shuttle
A damsel in force
A damsel in kitchen
A damsel full of resource
A damsel bleeding monthly
A damsel of draught
A damsel gives shelter
Another damsel zygote
A damsel of wit
A damsel of gut
A damsel of trust
Still A damsel but
Even if not in a brothel
She can be slanged Slut.

So in her progress
You can get a stinking smell
Not for any other reasons
But just because her being A damsel.
So you can mock her maturity
So you can mud her thick
So you can put her on fire
With petrol and matchstick

So you can weigh her worth
So you can regulate her fate
So you can decide how much freedom
She should exactly get !

So you can write her sentence
So you can throw her in dustbin
So you can kill her before birth
Earlier getting bone, flesh and skin.

I will tell you a story
A story of many damsels
Around all and sundry
Flying like Angels

In factories, In brothels
In fronts or in homes
They are the queens
Of their own Queendoms.

Some are having pistol in pockets
Some have pens in hands

Some design delicious dishes
With their magic wands.

Round their necks
Some have stethoscopes
Some are strict and strong
For usages of condoms.

I will not tell you the story anymore !
The fairy-tale of angels.
Look around you
The girl sitting next or near
May be one of those damsels.

RED SHOWCASE

The red showcase displaying human flesh,
With fake smile on lip, eyes of waiting eagerness.
Naked body in apparel of naked truth,
Mix together De Wallen, Sonagachi -- raw and uncouth.
Civilised cities of cultural heritage glitter at night
With their Red Light Zones in darkening bright.

Life lost and trapped unknowingly
In the trade of taxed, authorized profit.
Money rules, money buys, money forces
Customised love, serves lust 'the benefit'.

Loud lousy bodily beauty
With a silent, sorrowed soul.
Caged forever for desired freedom
To walk through the escape route
From the black-holed ghoul.
Earth revolves round the Sun
Seasons enter, exit too.
Days and nights fade into each other.
Red showcases remain unchanged
As an eternal zoo.

TOP VIEW

When I look down---

From the top most floor
Of the toppest construction
In this top-rated city.
I always feel fanned with
The pleasing breeze blows
Through the green lustrous beauty.
The view my eyes catch,
The mesmerised scenic
Often take my speech snatch.
I had been dreaming since my fifteen
To always be on the toppest
I had to prove a lot many times
The survival of the fittest.
And today this square of land I own,
Where I lavishly dwell.
I purchased this part of nature
To get lavishness unmatchable.
I have not only paid the price
But also made its value multiplied by thrice.

When I looked down---

From the top most floor
Of the toppest construction
In this top-rated city

I found my parents
In their doltish dotage
Deploring pity.
I found my children
Playing in dust
In torn clothes and hungry
When I tried finding
My wind chime, my woman
She seems loud and angry.
I daily run to stand first
In the queue of my daily wage,
Then take the baton for the next run
To barter for filling
The stomachs' rage.
I have been trying since my fifteen
To see the sky, to feel the breeze,
From a top most floor, to view lustrous green.
But probably for us nature ramparts herself
Who construct skeletons of skyscrapers
To be filled each square of her
With boastful and blind wealth-generators.
What else we can expect than our wages !
After all we are just labours.

SHOW OF SHOW-OFF

The hoardings with their high-held heads,
Are mirroring you across the city, your own place.
And what are you doing?
Visiting regularly the attic of your palace,
From the dump of debris.
Dragging an old iron chest,
Unlocking and lifting its lid,
Taking out an old broken mirror.
Dusting it's cracked glass,
With your soft white handkerchief.
Keening your cracked reflection in it.
Perhaps searching in the fractured self image!
The old and unbroken you.
Lost with time, with lost people, with lost moments.
The glossy flex hoardings,
Sometimes, somehow fail to show.
The reality behind the show-off.
Isn't so?

THE BOSS

I facewashed my wounds.
Buried the bruises
Under the deep layers
Of costly concealer.
I reddened my swollen lips
With the colouring hypocrisy.
Brand speaks from my brassiere to boots
The expense of fragrance hides
The cheap odour
Of the rotten corpse
I carry beneath my body.
Graved under my tormented mind!
I saw my self in the mirror
I saw the woman in me
Is ready again.

I shaved the boredom
Growing in shape of my beard
With full freedom.
Sprinkled the style
Over and over again
On my thicket tension, haired.
To overdo the mess, the unmaintained.
Brand speaks from my watch to waste belt.
But fails to tie the time
In my favour, with my favourite.
As I stood in front of the mirror

I saw the man in me
Is ready again.

We do ready us
For today, for tomorrow,
For another struggle.
For me, for us.
To Plunge into from,
One to another hollow.
With myself, crowned as
The high me, on high pedestals
Before me, before us.
The Boss.

OPIUM

I feel being loved by everyone.
I feel not being left alone.
I feel always being in a crowd.
I feel being remembered by the world.
I feel being with whom I want to be.
I feel my parents are not fighting in front of me.
I feel my universe is not torn apart.
I feel my entire galaxy is clear
Without a single pinch of dirt.

That's what I want to feel when I take the puff.
But how unfortunate, that even the puff also gives me
bluff.
And I become famous among you all as a frustrated soul.
Who tries to find an escape route with the help of a
ghastly ghoul.

Yes I am a drug addict who,
Seeks fortune in those powdered stuff.
But there must be a reason why have I stared to snuff !
To some extent it was myself with whom I couldn't cope
up.
But someone was there who,
Took me to that fire and helped me to jump.

The civilized society call them the peddlers.
Who are the mediums, who are the burglars.

Who sell the poison in the name of drugs.
Who trades with emotions being the thugs.

But to seal that treacherous way what does your society
do?
From where the poison comes and passes in the society
through!
Why you need to celebrate "The No Drug Day"?
Doesn't it seem like 'looking for a needle in the stack of
hay' !

Yes I am a drug addict and today I want to ask.
Though I know that blaming me is the most easy task.
But dear society, have you ever stood in front of the
mirror,
To answer this Quest ?
That even till today why your Law trusts,
 On the truth of a criminal spoken during his
'NARCOTIC TEST' ?

ALCOHOL

Consumption of Alcohol is injurious to health
Still liquor shops and pubs are prospering with wealth.
The person consuming alcohol framed as Alcoholic
But this word itself seems quite metaphoric !
Who never stairs up an wine shop,
Or never steps in a bar,
May be an alcoholic too
Somehow somewhere !

Alcohol of authority runs
To chase alcohol of power
Alcohol pleases processioning
Materialism's manner.
Alcohol of targeting ceaseless
The shameless success,
Few are consuming
Alcohol of - spitting bitterness.
Alcohol of social good
Alcohol of shouldering loads
Some are happy being alcoholic
Of chores overdose.

Alcohol circulates in veins
Of an entire nation
All countries and countrymen
Since the first step of civilisation.

WRITER'S BLOCKAGE

Few slice of pages I filled,
With few of my words--
Jammed or Buttered
With thousand thoughts
Few fiery, few chilled.
Few sugary, few peeper sprinkled.
Then, the words turned back.
Then, the thoughts stepped back.
With their hushed feet
They all gone forever.
Their departing notes said--
They need their wounds to be healed.
Wounds done by me
Provoking them to cross their extremity.
And here remained,
With a pen and few
Slice of empty pages new.
Wordless, Thoughtless
As if Soundless, Speechless.
I signed the mortgage
Without knowing
That I am in the
Well-known phase called,
"Writer's Blockage"

IF

---◆---

The world you live,
Doesn't belong to me.
The world I live,
Doesn't belong to you.
But still we dream
Still we hope,
If someday
Somehow
Our two hemispheres
Can shape a sphere!
With your desires,
With my dream.
If someday
Somehow....

If someday
Somehow....
We stop being scared
Of all our wars
We fought, we fight
Daily, forever...
And could come a new dawn
With a new start
When We two
Can shape an Us.
Will let love to spread.
Love will prevail

Love will speak
No social no legal
No boundaries to sneak
No one of us can ever claim
This is my world of fumed doom
And that is your world of fame
If someday
Somehow....

THE MIDNIGHT CALL (A Ballad)

I got down from the train,
It was a spooky midnight by that time.
The platform surface was dumb and empty,
Prevailing all-over a silence sublime.

Lonely, with the weighing luggage,
I was feeling a little weird.
A lonely girl !! In a lonesome place!!
Tired and little scared.

I made my mind to walk with my trolley,
Towards the entry of the city.
Without any unwanted element around me,
I felt placed in a zone of safety.

Only Few steps I could move ahead,
When few glaring lights blinded my vision.
A couple of motorbikes with six daring riders,
Appeared towards the station.

Soon, whistling horns started whirling round me,
A chilling fear wriggled in my spine,
Drops of freezing sweat started rolling down my neck,
I sensed my courage.....Decline!

I VERSOFICTION I

I tried to run and avoid the dirt;
But it was hard to avoid and run,
The dirt of creepy eyes and grip of masculine muscles
And the dirt of lousy words of fun.

My scream started to scratch the silence,
All and sundry at the midnight.
The Midnight stood as a silent listener,
Deaf, Mute and Blinded by fright.

My unresponsed shouts started mumbling,
Under the weight of masculinity on me
The weary soul started to stop thinking,
It was sure about losing its virginity

My deafening ears faintly heard,
 A sound of another approaching bike.
And soon, with its majestic Royalty,
An Enfield landed like a thunder strike.

To my almost crippling self-confidence,
That entry added a sense of stress,
My pleading body became extra alert,
To prepare for some extra scuffles.

My teary eyes caught a blurry vision,
Pair of three fast paced feet,
Advancing with their shadowy figures
Probably to take part in the delicious feast !

I was struggling still as an undefeated victim,
With my feminine clasping fists.

And feeding my drained guts with a faint fortitude--
That, I can not lose the battle like this.

A sudden thuds of kick and punch
Downpoured from back on the six hungry beasts
Were being busy in tearing the prey,
 The male lions became puzzle and freeze.

Three versus Six, an unequal fight,
But the melee made me baffled too !
Who arrived as my unexpected saviours?
My mind was gasping for clue.

The twisted tale ended with--
An aura of suspense.
The hoodlums vanished with--
Their bloody bruised faces.

My ripped off attire got a cover,
A black jacket from one of those three.
I was still not convinced of their motto !
They called off and arranged a taxi for me.

Perplexed I, finally summoned myself.
And asked for their introduction.
With such perfect dress code who they are?
In such midnight on road ! What is the intention?

 "Hi, I am Danny.
Hi, I am Sammy.
And Hi, my name is Paul.

You may be surprised to know-
That we are three Gigolos
Going to attend our Midnight Call."

PART-II
THE UNFINISHED FAIRYTALES

Collection of Twenty-Eight Poems on the theme of
Incomplete or Broken Love

REALM

Let me daydream of you
To get your glimpse in my dream.
Why to toil for the reality
Of your distancing from me !
When I know you were,
You are and will be forever
Nothing else but
Just only a dream...
Let me daydream of you
To get your glimpse in my dream.
There you will be cherished always
Let that only be our realm.

STORY TO TELL

All you have heard
Till now is--
A story about sleeping.
And I thought to tell you
A story of sleeplessness.
But I was wrong
That I forgot that,
All you have heard
Till now is—
Only the stories about
Just sleeping
Without the slightest sleeplessness.
So you will never understand
What eternal love is
As all you will be knowing,
Just the eternal slavery of
Mere physicalness.

TRACK

Being
"Off track" from me,
If keeps you "On track",
Then I will be.
Coz I am privileged
With prejudices for you.
What I have will have forever,
No one on this earth
Can ever have for you.
Being
"Off track" from me,
If keeps you "On track",
Then I will be.
Coz I am graced
With the grandeur of your love.
The love, never adored by thee.
But being your lover, I adorned all over me.

LONELY SKY

The shooting star is going back
To be seen in some other sky.
Where some eyes,
Still search and wait
For the shooting star.
To come, to grant,
The whispering wish
Of some awakened lips.
The shooting star is going back
To be seen, in that sky
It had left alone.
A long time back.

ONCE AS WE WERE

I still find you
In those dreams
I dream now daily.
Once upon a time
Which were our reality.
The reality, we dreamt for
The dream, we lived for.
Once upon a time
When you were there with me.
When I was there with you.
I still find you
In those dreams
I dream now daily.
Once upon a time
Which were our reality.

✻ PAUSALI MUKHERJEE ✻

ROASTED ROSE

The memories of our love
Are like the dried up petals
Of this rose, kept in the fold
Of this old poetry book.
Color-less, Smell-less
Yet full of feelings
Still so fresh !
Feelings which bring back
The fragranced memory of that day,
I gave you this rose and said--
"I love you, now tell me what do you say?"
Our story never moved on though..
So never my thoughts.
I bought this book
As your birthday present
The day you married your boss.

COLD WAIT

You may say that,
The longest night of the year,
Strict to follow the solar calendar.
But you are the Sun.
So you may not know !
But believe me, being the Moon I know,
That it comes each night,
Of every year..
When someone, somewhere
Keeps missing the presence
Of some another one,
May be living in some other where else.
May be with some other one !
The longest night of the year,
With a wave of cold wait,
Comes each night in every hemisphere.

ABYSS

Sometimes I feel
To climb the crest of my voice
To proclaim my love for you.
To let the world know
The downpour of feelings
Keeps me always drenched for you.
But then,,,
But then comes the domain.
Come the worlds then.
Where you live,
And where live I.
And makes me mum.
With my eyes dry,
And feelings dumb.
I see the endless abyss
There lies.
Between the globes of us two.
Between me and you.

PROP

Till now the number,
I wrote of poems are--
Five lac five thousand
Five hundred fifty five.
Whenever I sit,
With those worded pages--
I find the same line
Repeatedly I kept making live.
"I love you" was the word.
Each time with a new way.
How I kept on inscribing!
Every moment of every day.
Had they reached to your ears ever!
I wonder…!
Or have you ever tried to eavesdrop !
The answer perhaps a simple "NO" !
Or may be you were precious for me,
And I for you was just a prop !

RESTLESS REST

Do life waits for me
The way for you I wait?
Do time return gifts me
That special day
I and you met?
Do days and nights pass
The way they were spent by us?
When we stopped
Revolving ourselves,
To the world we belonged once,
Why this world is so restless
To take a second's rest?
That's all a broken heart always asks.

THE LOVE YOU TAUGHT

We came so close today.
An inch of gap only was there,
Between me and you.
Your eyes, fixed on me
I could sense !
But I kept mine downcast,
On my track as it was.
My heart, as always skipped a beat.
But from the other end
Of the window shield,
Was it possible to meet..!
You left my blind alley behind you,
With the trail of your engine smoke.
Smooth, Majestic, with the silent motion.
Just like the legacy you made of yourself.
I kept crawling with a 'nowhere to reach' notion.
And then I sensed that,
How deep, how far I have gone for you.
That I have also learnt to stir motionless.
That to remain calm in joy, 'in feel' emotionless.
Probably that is the Love,
You taught me to do !
Or I have only taught myself
With love, idolizing you...!

BODY'S SOUL

Soul never stops searching a body.
But does a body ever search for a soul?
One is incomplete without the other one.
But still the body remains stiff..!
Does it wait for the soul..!
To come and enthrone ?
So firm is the belief !
Of someone, on someone..!
Is it the eternal truth of love ?
Or we may say the eternal slavery !!
A prolonged process, so prominent.
Believe and keep believing.
On each, of every..!
Whoever are ever bound
In this unseen thread.
As a soul or sometimes as body
Have always acted.
The question may got tired or might doom .
Though Body and Soul both need each other.
But who fetches whom?

SMILEY

I just wanted to say
I love you.
I know you don't.
But still I do you.
The day my words for you ended,
I knew it was the last time
For me to feel you.
In those black words.
Like a blow of breeze,
It came sometimes though,
But fetching them, felt like--
Waiting in a queue.
Someone if asks me
Is it a break-up I did?
I am not sure what to say!
Though I had broken the worst,
But my heart never found the way--
To reach up to yours.
Just alike my blocked thoughts..
Who never found their alleys,
To free them from
The blind avenue of your memories.
Or probably the process is reciprocal..!
As you used to say sometimes.
When I always said, "I love you.."
And you replied through those yellow smiles.

❋ PAUSALI MUKHERJEE ❋

LISTEN-SILENT

One famous poet had said once—
In one of his poem,
On his lady's remembrance.
If to speak, there are many words,
Which no ear listens,
The best way the lip walks,
Is the path of silence.
But why to follow that path..!
That he never mentioned though.
It was understood by me,
When I afloat myself in your flow.
The flow of your thoughts and dreams,
Had scheduled me with rhymes wholesome,
The worldly worries forgot to toss me,
Or to flip the eventful pages of life's humdrum.
But then thee chose some unsung song.
To sing aloud without me along.
Then my thoughts numbed, words locked.
In an empty amphitheater, no ears to listen.
The best way my lips walked.
Was the snowy path of cold silence.
The famous poet told about what once.
In one of his poem,
On his lady's remembrance.

KORERO

--"Can we meet today?"
--"Sure we can."
--"And what else My Love?"
--"No followers or fan.
No guards, No barricades.
Neither in balls nor in masquerades.
A simple meet.
Of you with me.
Without your backdrops.
Under nature's serene canopy.
Can you come?
Or need time some?
Or there hides a 'NEI'..!
Beneath your 'WILL TRY'..
The best charming trick.
You kept playing on,
Since you made my PICK..!
I trust on a pure path.
As I belong from clarity.
It is you in a habit,
Of swirling the way sweetly.
But today let my destiny decide
Of which way to choose?
Can we meet today at the sunset point?
Or shall I wait for the match to loose?"

UNFINISHED

It could be a fairytale.
A story of a princess and her prince--
With lot many fairies around to bless and hail,
It could be their tale.

It could be a fairytale.
With garlands and bed of roses,
With an unending happiness,
To start with love and forever to prevail.
It could be their tale.
But it didn't happen so.
As the books didn't permit.
The books praised and prayed.
Through which could be seen God's reflect.

The same did the society where they stayed.
United in Preamble but in belief divided.
Hence with a shackle of institution,
The princess was caged.
And the charming prince!!
Somewhere was sentenced.
The story which could be their tale,
Remained as an Unfinished Fairytale,
Murdered, Burnt and Graved.

MARTYRED MARRIAGE

I never wanted to be back
To the city of this sunset
To that coop which was
Our home on rent.
I never wanted to be back
To the cage of these four walls.
Gifts grief like an abyss of darkness.
Someday was full with memories,
Of sunrays and fragrance.
But I had to today.
From the way back of graveyard.
Where with a Guard of Honor
A War deep soiled many like you,
And many like our marriages martyred.

✶ PAUSALI MUKHERJEE ✶

WHAT IF ?

What if..
Whatever she told
Is just a Lie?
What if..
Whatever she played on you
Is just a game?
What will you do?
When you will know them!
What will you do?
What if..! Who knows in fact..!
Whatever she did,
She did just to get you!
Now already you are her.
Won, Owned at every way.
Tell me please..
What will be done by you?
To her, whose hand you left.
Tell me please.
I am you..the inner you, slept.
What will be done to that home
To come out from which,
Whose door you broke?
What if.. ever again a chance you get
To enter through that broken door?
Will your footsteps to that way bend?
To that home, once again to mend?
Tell me please.

I am you..the inner you, slept.
What if..? If ever..?

UNEVEN EVE

———◆———

Under the cage of an Adam,
I was seeded as an Eve.
What was Almighty's plan for me?
Why this game of deceive?

I was my Rapunzel,
And my Cinderella.
In all my dreams in and out
I was only my Isabella.

Waiting to be kissed by a prince,
On every lonely night.
I kept my barren soul asleep,
Like the Snow White.

It was hard to recognize
Between a friend and foe
Warmth in all lippy smiles
And minds were full of snow.
In the desert of life,
Then came an oasis.
Like a delicious dessert,
Sweetens all my bitter crisis.

Man he was also,
With a soul of sage.

Or probably fool was I..!
Or my fate was full of rage!

For him I opened the cage,
Set my Eve in my Adam free.
But Alas! The soil couldn't produce the forbidden fruit,
That Adam wanted from the knowledge tree.

Family comes first for all
When arrives the acceptance moment
Social stature, respect, reputation
Stands taller than the tallest monument.

Wise I was but failed to realize.
With a success in surgery
I cannot change his search,
I cannot change me.

A woman freed from the cage of a man,
Powerful with constitution.
With equality and human rights in hand,
Accepted denial and humiliation.

Being an uneven Eve,
At the end of the day,
I learned, We, the Eves,
Wounded inside, with a smile on face
Can always accept dismay.

✻ PAUSALI MUKHERJEE ✻

EXTRA LOVE

Now you talk about honour !
Now you talk about duty !
Where were both of those then !
When your lust plunged into my naked beauty?

Now I am your mistake !
Now you care for your 'relation of ritual' !
Did you spend a moment even !
Before starting this game of betrayal ?

Now you find an escape route !
Taking refuge in the repute of your empire.
Why didn't your pondering pull you back !
When for me you left your partner ?

Probably I could have accept myself,
Even being considered as an extra.
I could have beam up my grief with,
Our rainbow moments and their spectra.

What was the need of this twist tale ?
The falsified game of blame !
If seducing a man would just be a woman's folly--
Then the hell love is not only blind, even lame.

I wonder what it was ?
A girl's true love without denial !

Or just few blatant intercoursing with a man !
Which The Constitution considers as Extra marital.

OATH

I never consider that
Falling for You.
Is a mistake I did.
But trying to bridge the gap !
Definitely was a disaster.
So I just stepped back myself.
With a promise to me
To not turn back again ever.
Some gaps need to be maintained.
Like a mountain and an abyss.
Forever distanced,
With an oath to meet never.
Let my quality time,
Be confined only in checking you
On a social store.
Let me fulfil my wish to see you
By peeping through the door.
Say what to be done after all..!!
All love can not be like storm and fire.
Let remain loves like mine and your,
Eternally incomplete as waves and shore.

YOU & I

You may stay on my lips like a poem
You may scatter in my breaths like fragrance
You may come and reside in my soul like love
And I...!!!
Being a beggar of you,
Eternally will be lost in your longing desire.
But keep my words,
I promise to not demand you from yourself.
My promises don't have any face of false words
They don't need also such one
Because they know how to smile even while bleeding.
You be you.
Stand on the top pedestal.
After all it's a pleasure for you to be on top always.
How can I restrict you from your happiness !
I love you after all !
So, Let me allow you to be there.
Let me allow myself to be lost in your longing desire
eternally.
Let me allow to make a promise.
That even being a beggar of you throughout,
I will never demand you from yourself.
Today I promise this to you.
Perhaps to myself too.

✻ PAUSALI MUKHERJEE ✻

THE THIRD EYE

On the towering top,
Of the dilapidated castle,
The first when we met.
I pinched myself
To feel the dream,
But unable to be felt.
It was like an austerity.
The toughest one,
The hardest one.
The cruellest one for me.
To ever chance my eyes
To please with thy magnetic vision.
To ever please my ears with your magical baritone.
In which you whispered my name !
It was like the dizzy dream
Anyone dreams sleeping,
During an hour alluring.
Of deep satisfaction.
Under the coolest shade of a huge green tree.
Like sleeping on your mother's lap.
Being old as a babbling bee.
But then broke my dream.
As the not so good God and Goddess,
Opened their third eyes.
And I saw my own reflection
In that fire that brightly shines.
The fire of truth.

The truth I often shelved.
My shelved identity--
Not possible to be denied.
I shrank, I withdrawn.
But it was too late by then.
Your thick lips locked mine thin petals and mixed.
Your left arm made my waist chained.
And the right one foraged.
For that special part private--
An eternal search whenever
An Adam meets an Eve.
And then you felt--
The fright I saw in your eyes.
To be cheated, to be shattered.
I know how it feels.
I have felt the same unnumbered times many.
If desired someone only for me,
For being my lover, for now, for eternity.
Not only I, We, the all We.
The creation of the third eyes
Of the not so good God and Goddess.
We the merged selves.
Of the Nature and the Male.
The two basic, opposite.
Independent and eternal.
Whom you slanged
Fuck ! Eunuch !
And gone. Forever.

Mr. Gloomy Grey AND Ms. Restless Rainbow

A stroke of hue from her pallet,
Could colour any gloomy day.
She was Ms. Restless Rainbow,
Who fell in love with Mr. Grey.
Mr. Grey was the colour of gloom,
Which Ms. Rainbow kept on brightening.
But no one has ever tried to know,
What costs her for this colouring!

Days when everything was gloomy around him,
She tried to turn them into cheer.
No one ever asked her ever,
What she had to go through then!
What she had to bear!!

She spreads smile always,
And never uttered a complaint.
And no one was interested to find out,
What her smile really meant!

All the gloom of Mr. Grey's world,
She absorbed within her.
And painted the walls around him
With her own VIBGYOR.
She obsessed herself so much-
With the love of Mr. Grey,

That she started becoming colour-blind,
At the 'end of the day'.

Mr. Grey has now completely coloured.
Except his name, everything is changed.
Red, Blue, Yellow, Green and many more colours are there,
Who always now keep him encircled.

But Ms. Restless Rainbow is nowhere to be seen!
Neither no one knows where she is now!
That world has left her alone,
Which once she coloured with her hue.

May be for a while she turns pale and fade,
But Restless Rainbows can never vanish.
By the absorbed gloom from Grey,
The enormous energy within her can never finish.

She is the powerhouse of colour,
With her own charm and vivacity.
Completely excluding her from mind!
Mr. Grey doesn't have that capacity.

In the crowd of encircling colours
Sometimes he also misses,
That enigmatic aura of VIBGYOR.
Out of reach even after several searches!

This doesn't happen with every love-story,

No need to fear.
Mr. Gloomy Grey and Ms. Restless Rainbow,
Are to be found very rare.

LOVE DOMAIN

His mansion is few steps from my hut,
I see it on my way.
I tend to turn my feet once to him,
Almost every day.

The mansion is in public domain,
Without a guard at gate.
But to avail all domains publicly !
Few public are not so fortunate.

I wished to meet him once all alone,
Tried, if my dream could come true !
But as he's always in public domain,
Alas! My wish didn't reach through.

Unnumbered times it happened like that,
My heart opened its gate to welcome him.
But being in public domain, he couldn't make out to come,
All his trials became a failed aim.
Being in public domain isn't so easy you know!
There, morning tea comes with a TV bite,
Flex and Hoarding do Mirror's work,
Around the city you're on sight.
How would I know what it means!
When I've never lived so publicly!
How would I know how it feels!

Being a frog in my well of privacy!

I will surely ask God few questions.
Does domain really matter?
God is in the most public domain I hope.
Hopefully He will not flatter.

When God has time to meet his devotees,
Then why not we humans?
Why we keep building our card-castles,
With scheduled busyness of illusion?

Why love needs to check and choose?
Between mansions and huts?
Between public and private?
Between shame and guts?

THE UNTYING

We tied the knot of trust
We tied the knot of respect
We tied the knot of love
All untied. No regret.

The untying was sacred
As much as the tying was
The holy oaths turned profane
And paled the perfume pious.

Was it my mistake?
Or it was your choice!
Did your ego fan the fire?
Giving onlookers rejoice!

Answers are unknown
Unlikely to be solved
Few questions should remain forever
Detained and not dissolved.

A broken marriage, a broken love
May untie two people
Rituals may not receive rapture
Gossips may giggle.

But the final untying
Waits till the date

 PAUSALI MUKHERJEE

When we hear the supreme call
And from our physiques, our souls dissect.

GRAVED LOVE

In this emotionless heat,
Our cold distanced lives
Are melting down slowly; daily.
And love..!! already we have
Graved that long time ago.
I never considered that,
Falling for You.
Is a mistake I did.
But trying to bridge the gap !
Definitely was a disaster.
Stepping back myself
For not turning back again.
Was all I could do to redress.
Some gaps need to be maintained.
Like a mountain and an abyss.
Like the sky and earth.
Always and forever distanced.
Let in the heat of stolidity
This cold distance between us,
Burn into ashes forever.
Like those cherished dreams.
Which we already had epitaphed,
Long time ago with our love, graved.

<u>28</u>
<u>WAVE AND SHORE</u>

In small towns few names are so big.
Wherever you may go,
Breeze will whisper them in your ears.
On each tree you will find birds,
Singing those names sitting on a twig.
Escape route you may try myriads.
Thy will come across to cross your way,
With the beam of their boast like a prig.
In a small town few names are really big.
If you fall for such a big name in a small town.
Better fake your smile, let heart sigh, hurt and frown.
Better let your quality time be confined only-
In checking that big name on a social store.
It may feel just like to look something at-
Peeping through the closed slides of door.
What to do after all..!
No regret, all love can not be like storm and fire.
Let some love also be like waves and shore.

PART- III

BIG SHORTS

There is a difference between micro and mini. These are all mini tales, total 9 in number on different themes.

PATRIARCHY

"Dear Mumma,

I love you both but I can't stop loving Rehaan too. Tell the man of our home that I am leaving home.

-Your loving Rishu."

At 2.30 a.m. the mobile police van rescued an injured half-naked senseless young man from the highway side. He was admitted to the nearby hospital and declared to be brutally penetrated… Anally. Probably more than fifteen times.

A week later Mrs. Shrivastava got a call and were informed to come ASAP.

On the hospital bed, the young man received a note. "Rishu,

We both love you very much. The man of the home will accept and love whoever the other man of the same home will love.

-Pappa."

Mr. Shrivastava entered into the cabin. Tightly hugging him, his only son Rishav told, "You don't have to accept and love anyone except me. I love you Pappa. Please take me home."

PATRIOTS

"My girlfriend is scared of cockroach."

"Hahahaha and mine one is of lizard."

"What about yours Anwaar..?"

"We married last week only. Now she is only scared of losing me."

A chit of chat in the mid of a tiny tea-break during the night patrolling duty proves that nowadays tension is a bit less…may be!

A sudden gunning started from the other side of the dark mountains. As a bolt from the blue, two soldiers saw their one week old new team-mate Anwaar's bloody dead body steadily falling on the ground.

Next day morning the newspaper headline was of some famous personality's statement that 'Patriotism depends on religion'. The small death incident of three patriots Girdhaari, Anwar and Joseph in a sudden gunfire in Batalik sector was nowhere to be found in any newspaper though.

KOHL

"Class 12 students shouldn't miss their Physics class Ma'am..!" replied the Principal Mrs. Furnandez.

With a weary mind and eyes tired of a whole night weeping, Gunjan entered the classroom.

"Fuck off your eyes!!"… said Abhik furiously today morning after giving her a tight slap. But, she saw it..! How could she disbelief her eyes? Yesterday afternoon Abhik and a girl were sexing on the same bed, on which Gunjan and Abhik sleep in every night..together…since their four years of marriage.

While coming out of the classroom, the last bench boy handed a chit to Gunjan.

"May be you don't believe but I believe that on this earth, you have the most beautiful eyes. Don't ever forget to apply KAJAL Ma'am

--Himanshu."

Gunjan left Abhik but She never left putting Kajal on her eyes after that day.

Himanshu left the city for further study.

PARANORMAL

Obsessed with the mysterious man in her dream, Pihu came today to the dilapidated fort on the hill-top. But her believe of meeting someone there, gone in vain. It was getting dark. She had to go back to her rented coop soon. She searched for her mobile to book a cab. It was not there in the bag. Panicked due to the incomprehensible loss, Pihu re-entered inside the skeleton of the ruins for the search of her mobile. The darkness gobbled her inside it. Her sleep broke. She opened her eyes. Found her body down the broken stairs lying in a pool of blood with a bag of fractured bones. She felt a light touch a on her shoulder. She turned and saw her dream-man standing there with a smile.

(This is a work of Fiction. Ghosts do not exist.)

THE WHORE

"You won't believe what a body that whore has!! Just as smooth as butter!! As tasty as honey…!! What I suggest that in a lifetime at least once you all should visit her… I will share her number in our office group."

During the lunch hour Aniket was sharing with his close group of office buddies about his last night's experience with a high profiled escort.

Shantanu giggled and said "You all may need that number, but I don't want. At least not for the next five year. Ask me why?"

A light loud manly roar -- "WHY????"

"The item I got to taste permanently before two weeks, is the best butter and honey I have tasted yet….That's why."

At that night during the love making moments, Arpita couldn't even realize that how she has transformed as a market-whore; few more manly hands are either masturbating or intercoursing, thinking about her; that day during lunch hour, her two weeks old husband has shown all her nudes he has clicked till date, to his close group of office buddies.

MAGMA

An exquisite Bone China dish hurled out from the Antique Mehgani table on the uncarpeted Italian marble floor.

With utter disgust and abusive fury few heavy footfalls of

a pair of leather boots walked out of the main door to attend a seminar on "Stress Handling". There on the Persian carpet, the scattered mess of salt less slices of buttered bread and scrambled egg smirked at each other when with eyes filled with salty tears a female hands started collecting them. Today again she forgot 'to salt' the morning meal of her husband, Mr. Arghyadeep Basu, the most renowned "Anger Management Coach" of the town.

✻ PAUSALI MUKHERJEE ✻

THE GREEN LIGHT

Since a month Kishore has been doubting that Neha is cheating on him. On the way back from office, a fiery conversation is ongoing even today. The green light beside Neha's name went off abruptly. Kishore not even noticed. The radio is saying, time is exact 7.00 in the evening. The green light of the traffic signal turned red. The race of all the running trails of expensive and non-expensive tires stops for a while. With his eyes closed, Kishore relaxed himself on the back seat of the hired cab. He is actually fade up of this live-in, literally tired.

That late evening, with the help of the neighbors, when an exhausted Kishore finally broke the door of his rented coop, his relationship was broken already. Neha was staring at the small crowd with her vision less sight, in the drawing room, hanging from the ceiling fan.

Three years of knowing each other finally ended in three months court trial where it was proved that Neha was a suicidal and Kishore was really innocent.

Now whenever Kishore sees the green light in the traffic stand, the vision of Neha's postmortem report with the death timing between 7 to 7.30 p.m., flashes in his vision. That day when the green light in traffic became red and the green light beside Neha's messenger profile extinguished forever.

HONOUR KILLER

The message was short but it shot exact as a sniper.
Advocate. Devesh Mehra was hemorrhaged and agitated
of this idea of revenge. He and his entire empire will
completely be uprooted if now in this peak of his career
he is being charged under the trending storm of "#metoo".
He dialed Shailendra. His true confidant.
"A tragic accident of a family of three. The small car
smashed by a juggernaut."
The short column published in few leading newspapers
about an accident occurred last night on the National
Highway, brought a crooked smirk on Mitra's face. He
finally deleted the message of his ex-employee Ratna
where she had confessed that though she loves Devesh
more than herself and all the physical moments between
them are her lifelong treasure but to save her marriage and
daughter, she is now left with no option than accepting
her husband's proposal of filing a case of sexual
harassment against Devesh.
Shailendra got a text--"Thanks Bro."
"Anything for your honour."—he replied to Devesh.

WOLFISH

In past eight months, including the last one of S.I. Kripanath Bohral, eight mysterious and horrific murders have not only shaken the peaceful core of the 'Hill-Queen' with tremor but also have left the entire department with no clue except that all victims are the S.I of Sukhpokhria Police Station and are killed ruthlessly by some anonymous animal nearby or inside the S.I. Bungalow.

Being the one month old, newly stationed S.I. of this calaboose, Ms. Avika Gaur is assigned as the new in-charge of the case as expected.

The interval of exact 15 days is signaling towards a doubt which Avika can only understand. Though now she has completely tamed herself but her inner being has started signaling that full moon is approaching fast. She has already applied for two days leave and planned to send Roopchand, the all-in-one domestic help, to a leave for a couple of days. She can't risk an innocent life.

The full moon is galvanizing the panoramic night view of the sloppy, hilly terrain with its silver beam.

Inside the S.I. Bungalow, one male is finally mating with a female version of his species. Two warewolves. Roopchand and Avika.

(This is a work of Fiction. Warewolves do not exist.)